"Where Do All The Birds Go When It Rains?"

Written by:
Misty Hoopman

Illustrated by:
Joshua Allen

AuthorHouse™
1663 Liberty Drive
Bloomington, IN 47403
www.authorhouse.com
Phone: 833-262-8899

This book is printed on acid-free paper.

ISBN: 978-1-4918-6191-2 (sc)
ISBN: 978-1-4918-6192-9 (e)

Library of Congress Control Number: 2014902389

Print information available on the last page.

Published by AuthorHouse 07/22/2023

authorHOUSE

To: Abby, Adam and Azalea

Acknowledgment

I was inspired to write this book for my love of animals and children. I began writing it a couple years back when I was living in Austin, Texas. I was constantly seeing birds everywhere in the city and off of the freeways. I often thought to myself where do all of the birds go when it rains? My mother, Christine has done in-home child care for over twenty-five years now so I grew up around children. She has been an inspiration in my life.

I met my husband Gabe in July of 2013 and we are now happily married with two children, Alexandra and Sydney. He has been the one that has helped make this dream into a reality and I thank him with my whole heart!

Where do all of the birds go?

You can search high and low,
but when it rains we just don't know.

Some birds fly high up in the sky,
above the clouds to keep dry.

Some hide up in the trees,
while others take cover under the leaves.

Some take quick showers,
while others bathe in great big flowers.

Some birds eat,
while others sleep.

Some wash their beaks,
while others wash their feet.

Some rest in their nests,
while others puff up their chests.

Some huddle together,
to stay warm in this weather.

When the raindrops start to slow,
perhaps a rainbow will begin to show.
There are many birds to be found,
if you just know where to look around!

Thank you very much for reading my book.
I hope you enjoyed it as much as I enjoyed writing it!

Please visit my website at:
www.hoopmanbooks.com

Misty Hoopman

Printed in the United States
by Baker & Taylor Publisher Services